Alone
Together

Suzanne Bloom

BOYDS MILLS PRESS

AN IMPRINT OF HIGHLIGHTS

Honesdale, Pennsylvania

Text and illustrations copyright © 2014 by Suzanne Bloom

Boyds Mills Press, Inc.
815 Church Street
Honesdale, Pennsylvania 18431
boydsmillspress.com
Printed in China
ISBN: 978-1-62091-736-7
Library of Congress Control Number: 2014931586

First edition
10 9 8 7 6 5 4 3 2 1

Production by Margaret Mosomillo
The text of this book is set in ITC Legacy Sans.
The illustrations are done in pastel.

To Rick and Eileen, since forever

Where's Bear?   Over there.

Alone?

Sometimes,
Bear likes to be alone.

Me, too.
I'm going to be alone with Bear.

Why are you all by yourself, Bear?
Are you sad?
Are you mad?
Are you lonely?

Occasionally, I like some quiet time.

Me, too.

Quiet leaves room for humming.

Hmmmmmm.

Hmmmmmm.

Hmmmmmm.

And twirling.

And whooshing like the wind.

Whoosh!

I mean hush! No noise! Quiet! Please.

I'm a little lonely over here, all by myself.
Are you done being alone, Bear? *Hmm?*

Hmmmmm.
Hmmm.
Hmm.

Yes. I guess.
You'll be quiet?

As quiet as a
little sleeping fox.

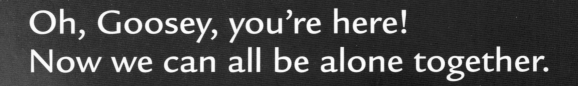

Oh, Goosey, you're here!
Now we can all be alone together.